by Jo Harper • *pictures by* JoAnn Adinolfi

Outrageous, Bodacious

Boliver Boggs!

S.M.B.S.D.

SIMON & SCHUSTER BOOKS FOR YOUNG READERS

SIMON & SCHUSTER
BOOKS FOR YOUNG READERS
An imprint of Simon & Schuster
Children's Publishing Division
1230 Avenue of the Americas
New York, New York 10020

Text copyright © 1996 by Jo Harper
Illustrations copyright © 1996
by JoAnn Adinolfi

SIMON & SCHUSTER BOOKS FOR YOUNG READERS
is a trademark of Simon & Schuster.
Book design by Heather Wood
The text for this book is set in Stymie Medium.
The illustrations are rendered in gouache, watercolors,
pastels, and pastel pencil on watercolor paper.
Printed and bound in Hong Kong
by South China Printing Co. (1988) Ltd.
First Edition
1 3 5 7 9 10 8 6 4 2

Library of Congress Cataloging-in-Publication Data
Harper, Jo.
Outrageous, bodacious Boliver Boggs!
by Jo Harper ; pictures by JoAnn Adinolfi.
p.   cm.
Summary: Boliver Boggs spins outrageous excuses
for being late to school, and these tall tales provide hilarious
entertainment to the students in Miss O'Brien's class.
ISBN 0-689-80504-7
[1. Punctuality—Fiction. 2. Schools—Fiction. 3. Tall tales.]
I. Adinolfi, JoAnn, ill. II. Title.
PZ7.H23135Th 1996 [E]—dc20 95-6029 CIP AC

For *Josephine*,
child of my right hand
—J. H.

For *Nana and Pop*,
who filled my childhood
with treasures of the heart and mind
that I shall carry with me always
—J. A.

When anything went wrong, Boliver Boggs always had a whopping good excuse.

One morning his teacher, Miss O'Brien, said, "Boliver Boggs, you are one hour late. That is outrageous."

Boliver Boggs said, "Yes, ma'am, you're plumb right about that. What you say is the pure-d truth, but this morning I come up against an exceptional circumstance."

The other students in Miss O'Brien's class grinned. "On with the story, Boliver Boggs!" they shouted.

"Miss O'Brien," began Boliver Boggs, "the truth is I left home early because I thought I might be able to give you a hand with some of your classroom chores. I moseyed right along, practicing my multiplication tables. When I got near the thicket where the wild roses grow, my eye fell on an extraordinary sight. On the sidewalk in front of me lay two humongous snakes—a brown one and a yellow one.

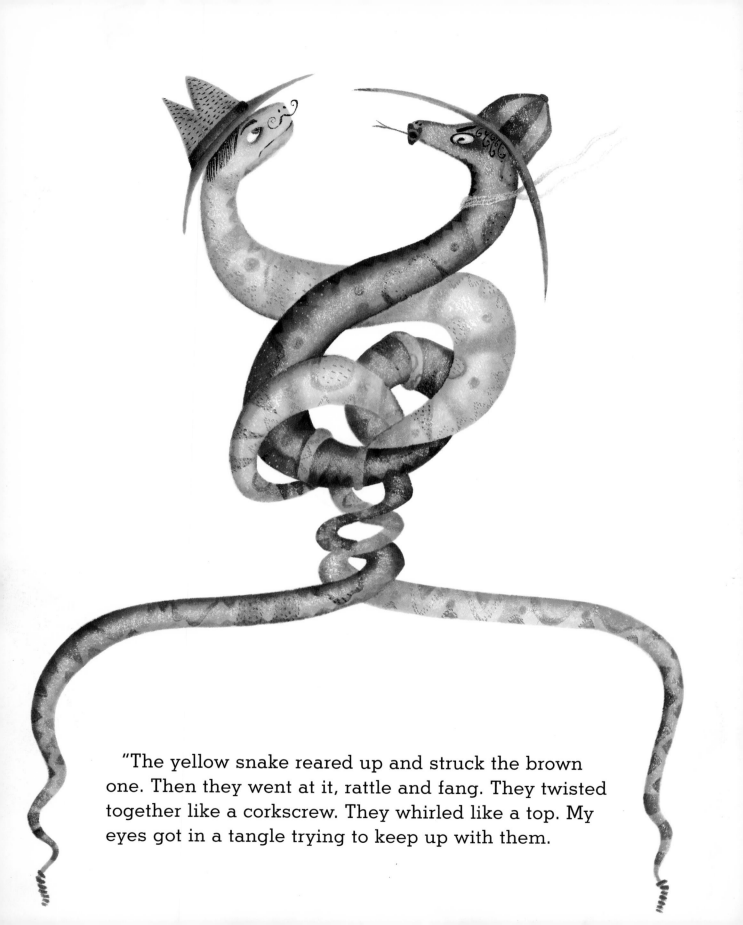

"The yellow snake reared up and struck the brown one. Then they went at it, rattle and fang. They twisted together like a corkscrew. They whirled like a top. My eyes got in a tangle trying to keep up with them.

"Suddenly I realized that I was fixing to be late. It seemed only fitting that I bring a little something in hand to show why I was tardy. I wanted to prove that what I was saying was a dead open fact. So I sneaked up and snatched the yellow's rattler.

"Then I streaked it. . . .

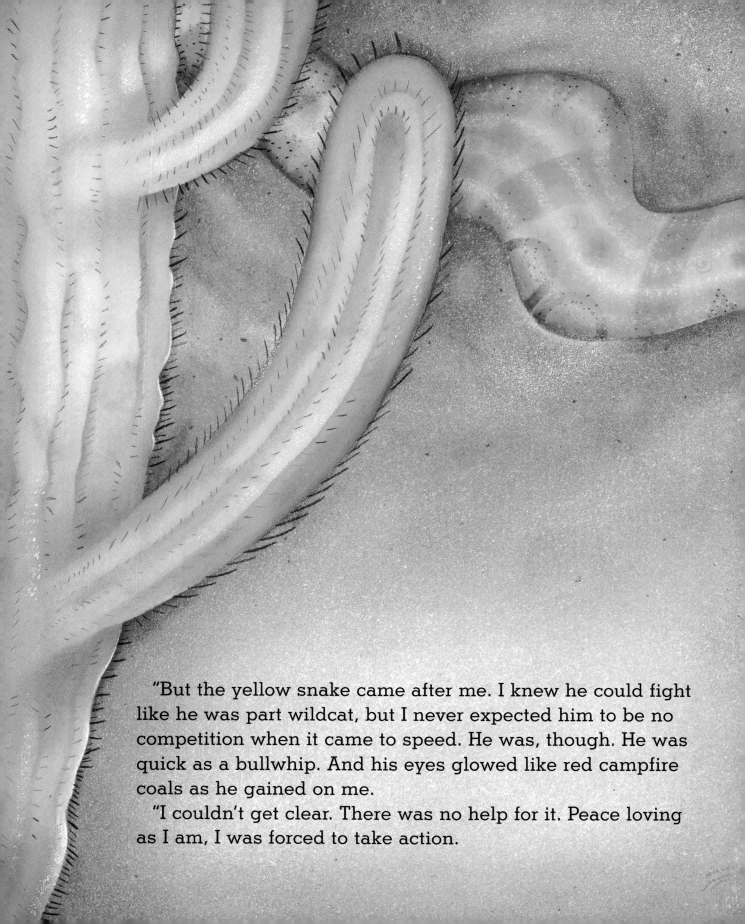

"But the yellow snake came after me. I knew he could fight like he was part wildcat, but I never expected him to be no competition when it came to speed. He was, though. He was quick as a bullwhip. And his eyes glowed like red campfire coals as he gained on me.

"I couldn't get clear. There was no help for it. Peace loving as I am, I was forced to take action.

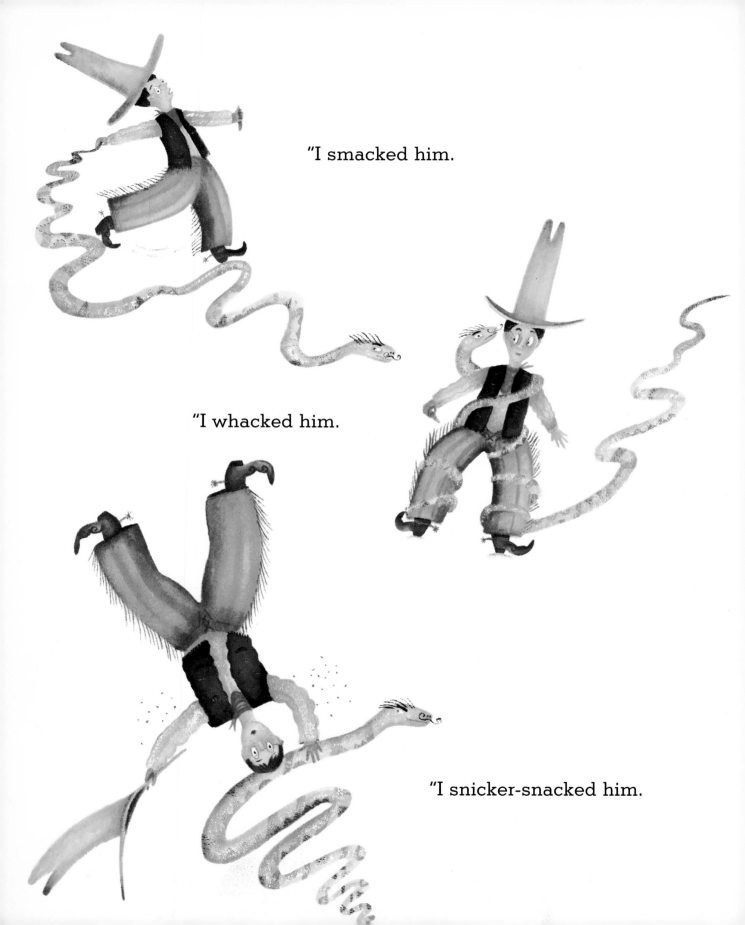

"I smacked him.

"I whacked him.

"I snicker-snacked him.

"I tossed him in a loop and rolled him like a hoop. I would have rolled him to school, but he slipped down a drain, and dag-nab, if I didn't drop the rattle down, too.

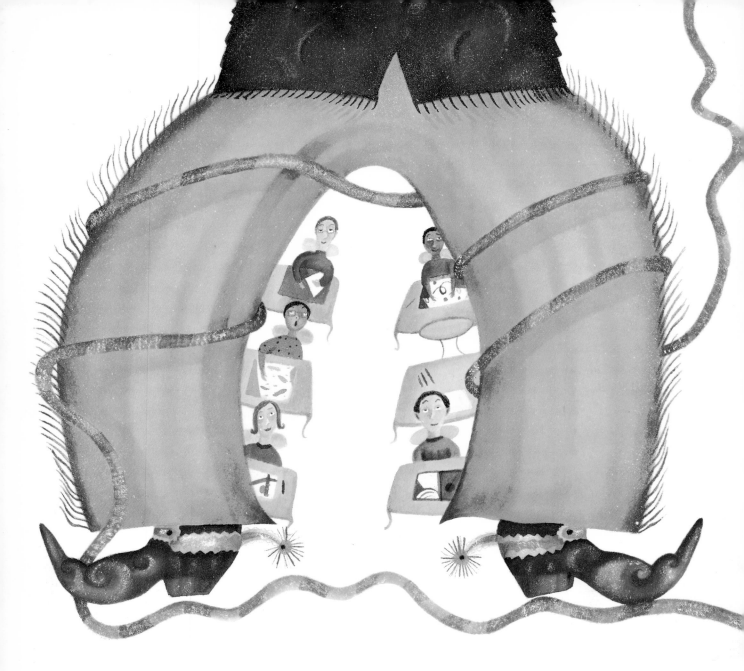

   "That's why I'm late. It's the honest truth, just as sure as you're breathing."
   Miss O'Brien sighed.
   And the students said, "You're outrageous! You're bodacious! You're whopperiferous, Boliver Boggs!"
   Boliver Boggs grinned and clunked to his seat in his cowboy boots.

The very next morning Boliver Boggs was late again. Miss O'Brien said, "Boliver Boggs, you are one hour late. That is outrageous."

Boliver Boggs said, "Yes, ma'am, you're plumb right about that. What you say is the pure-d truth, but I come up against an exceptional circumstance."

The students' faces brightened. "On with the story, Boliver Boggs!" they shouted.

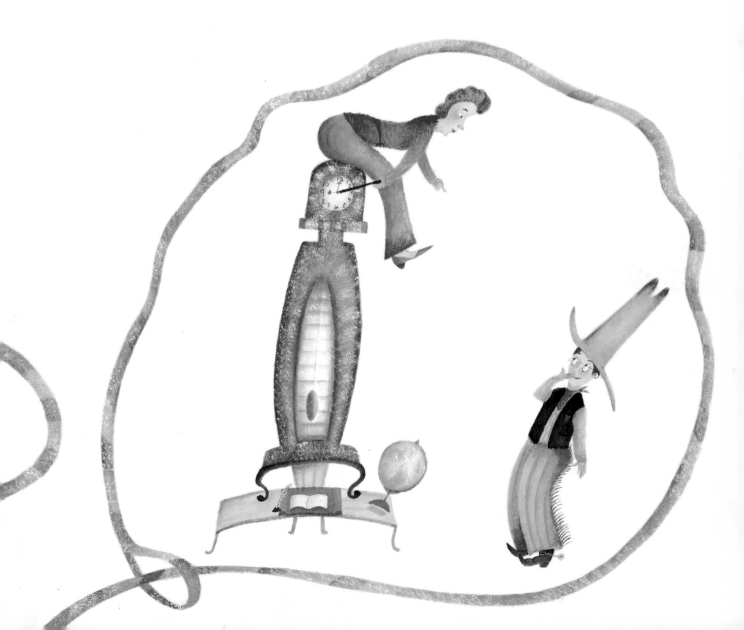

"Miss O'Brien, I know how you hate for me to be late, so this morning I turned at the thicket where the wild roses grow and took a shortcut through the woods. I was sniffing the fresh morning air and skipping through the dew when a bear reared up right in front of me.

"Ma'am, I know disaster when it's staring me in the face, so
I turned tail and ran, but the bear grabbed me from behind.

"I wiggled and twisted, but he stuck as close to me as a turtle to his shell. That bear hugged me like a brother. I couldn't break loose, and he was squeezing me into pressed ham.

"That squeeze inspired me with mortal fear, and nothing
can give you a dose of super strength the way mortal fear can.
I fought that bear like he was my equal, and sometimes I
thought I wouldn't make it.

"Finally he fetched me a blow that knocked all the compassion
out of me. That's when . . .

"I would have brought him to school, but I knew his teeth would scare the little kids.

"And that's why I'm late. It's the honest truth, just as sure as you're breathing."

Miss O'Brien sighed.

And the students said, "You're outrageous! You're bodacious! You're whopperiferous, Boliver Boggs!"

Boliver Boggs grinned and clunked to his seat in his cowboy boots.

The next morning Boliver Boggs was late again. Miss O'Brien said, "Boliver Boggs, you are one hour late. That is outrageous."

Boliver Boggs said, "Yes, ma'am, you're plumb right about that. What you say is the pure-d truth, but this morning I come up against an exceptional circumstance."

The students in Miss O'Brien's class clapped and cheered. "On with the story, Boliver Boggs!"

"This morning when I got to the thicket where the wild roses grow, they looked so pretty that they brought you to mind, Miss O'Brien. So I commenced picking you a bouquet.

"I hadn't hardly got started when I felt something watching me. I didn't know what, and I didn't know where, but I could sense strange eyes.

"My neck began to prickle and my skin began to crawl. I looked all around, but there wasn't nothing in sight. Then I heard a rustling. I looked down. Something was twitching on the ground.

"It was long.
"It was speckled.
"It was prickly.

"I couldn't figure out what it was, but I was bound and
determined to find out, so I went tiptoeing to where it led me.

"Well, I was tiptoeing on a tail! And that tail hooked onto the weirdest critter I ever did see.

"It had a mane like a lion, and horns like a bull, and it was standing there smelling the roses. Miss O'Brien, I was bumfuzzled.

"Then it come to me that I was heading down the late trail again. I lit out so fast, I stubbed my toe and dropped your bouquet, and I didn't take time to pick it up."

Miss O'Brien sighed.

Suddenly, all the students gasped. "Look!" they shouted.
Miss O'Brien said, "What an extraordinary circumstance!"
And for once, Boliver Boggs didn't say a word. He was
surprised speechless.

The End